DATE DUE

Encyclopedia Brown

Cracks the Case

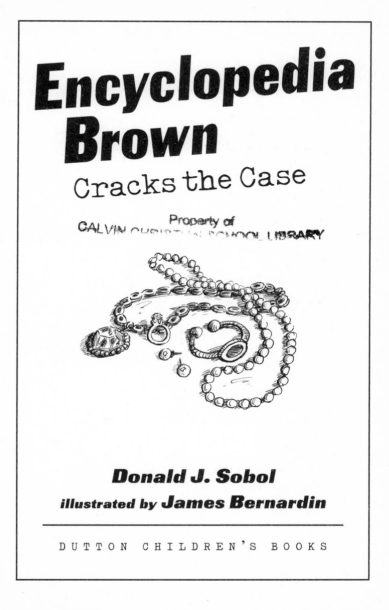

Donald J. Sobol

illustrated by James Bernardin

DUTTON CHILDREN'S BOOKS

DUTTON CHILDREN'S BOOKS
A division of Penguin Young Readers Group

Published by the Penguin Group
Penguin Group (USA) Inc., 375 Hudson Street, New York, New York 10014, U.S.A. • Penguin Group (Canada), 90 Eglinton Avenue East, Suite 700, Toronto, Ontario M4P 2Y3, Canada (a division of Pearson Penguin Canada Inc.) • Penguin Books Ltd, 80 Strand, London WC2R 0RL, England • Penguin Ireland, 25 St Stephen's Green, Dublin 2, Ireland (a division of Penguin Books Ltd) • Penguin Group (Australia), 250 Camberwell Road, Camberwell, Victoria 3124, Australia (a division of Pearson Australia Group Pty Ltd) • Penguin Books India Pvt Ltd, 11 Community Centre, Panchsheel Park, New Delhi - 110 017, India • Penguin Group (NZ), 67 Apollo Drive, Rosedale, North Shore 0745, Auckland, New Zealand (a division of Pearson New Zealand Ltd) • Penguin Books (South Africa) (Pty) Ltd, 24 Sturdee Avenue, Rosebank, Johannesburg 2196, South Africa • Penguin Books Ltd, Registered Offices: 80 Strand, London WC2R 0RL, England

Text copyright © 2007 by Donald J. Sobol
Illustrations copyright © 2007 by James Bernardin

CIP Data is available.

Published in the United States by Dutton Children's Books,
a division of Penguin Young Readers Group
345 Hudson Street, New York, New York 10014
www.penguin.com/youngreaders

Designed by Jason Henry

Printed in USA • First Edition
ISBN: 978-0-525-47924-6
10 9 8 7 6 5 4 3 2 1

For Joe Cirulli

CONTENTS

The Case of the Forgetful Jewel Thief

To most people, Idaville looked like many seaside towns. It had four banks, three movie theaters, and two delicatessens. It had churches and synagogues and lovely white beaches.

But Idaville only *looked* like other seaside towns.

For more than a year, no grown-up or child in Idaville had gotten away with breaking the law. Police officers across the nation wondered how Idaville did it. What was the secret?

Only three people knew the answer to that question, and they weren't telling.

All three lived in a red brick house at 13

Rover Avenue—Mr. Brown, Mrs. Brown, and their only child, ten-year-old Encyclopedia, America's best crime-buster.

Mr. Brown was Idaville's chief of police. He was honest, brave, and smart. Whenever he had a case that seemed impossible to solve, he always did the same thing. He went home to dinner. Encyclopedia usually would solve the case with just one question. Usually before dessert.

Police chiefs across America believed that Mr. Brown was the best police chief in the world. Chief Brown was proud of his record and proud of his officers. But he had to keep his pride in Encyclopedia a secret. Who would believe that a fifth-grader was the real mastermind behind Idaville's war on crime?

So he said nothing.

Encyclopedia never bragged about the help he gave to his father. He didn't want to seem different from other fifth-graders.

But he was stuck with his nickname.

Only his parents and teachers called him by

his real name, Leroy. Everyone else in Idaville called him Encyclopedia.

An encyclopedia is a book or set of books filled with all kinds of facts from *A* to *Z*. Encyclopedia had read more books than anyone in Idaville, and he never forgot what he read. He was the only walking library in America.

One Friday evening at the dinner table, Encyclopedia poked his salad with his fork, searching for raw onions. There weren't any.

Chief Brown sat staring at his salad instead of eating it.

Encyclopedia and his mother knew what that meant. A case had Chief Brown puzzled. Encyclopedia leaned back. He waited for his father to speak.

At last Chief Brown put down his fork.

"We caught a jewel thief this morning coming out of Von Martin's Fine Jewelry Store right here in Idaville. He's the same man who has been robbing stores all over the state," he said.

Mrs. Brown and Encyclopedia had both read

about the robber in the newspaper. A number of stores in their part of the state had been hit.

The thief would tell the salesperson that he was looking for an expensive gift for his elderly mother. As soon as the store clerk opened the jewelry cases, the thief grabbed the most expensive jewels and ran. Priceless pieces had disappeared into his pockets.

"But you caught the thief, dear. I wonder why you don't sound happy," Mrs. Brown said, rubbing her eyes.

"Mr. von Martin got his jewelry back," Chief Brown explained. "And we have clear pictures of the thief from security cameras in other stores. We know he's guilty, but the thief says he can't remember where he hid the jewels from his other robberies. I spent all afternoon questioning him, but he didn't give up any clues."

"I'm sure Leroy can help you solve the case." Mrs. Brown sniffed and rubbed her eyes again. "My eyes sting," she said. "Were the jewels very valuable?"

"Yes," Chief Brown said with a sigh. "The

very first store he robbed didn't have insurance. The owners will be ruined if we don't get their jewels back."

"Could the thief have a partner?" Mrs. Brown asked. "Could he have given the jewels to his mother?"

Encyclopedia listened carefully as his mother spoke. He knew she was asking questions so he would have all the facts.

Chief Brown said, "She was terribly shocked when she heard her son had been arrested. She seems like a nice woman. I don't think she's involved."

"Have you searched the thief's home?" Mrs. Brown asked.

"We've gone over every inch," Chief Brown said. "We found pictures of jewelry, books about jewelry, and maps of towns with jewelry stores in them. But no jewels."

Mrs. Brown glanced at Encyclopedia. He wasn't ready to ask his one question, so she continued. "What about his car?"

"There was nothing in his car, except some

letters he hadn't gotten around to mailing to his mother." Chief Brown patted his pocket. "He even asked if he could write her another one after lunch this afternoon."

"Are there clues in the letters?" Mrs. Brown asked.

"Not that we can tell," Chief Brown answered. "Perhaps he really doesn't remember where he hid the jewels."

"Hmmm," Mrs. Brown said thoughtfully. "If I was that forgetful, I would write things down. Perhaps the letters are written in code." Mrs. Brown coughed. She was too polite to ask the biggest question on her mind—and up her nose. "Read the letters to Leroy," she urged. "He's broken codes before."

Mrs. Brown looked at her son again. The boy detective had closed his eyes and taken a deep breath. He always closed his eyes when he did his deepest thinking. Suddenly his eyes opened.

Encyclopedia asked the question his mother

wanted to. "How come you *stin* . . . er, smell so awful, Dad? What's that smell?"

Mrs. Brown seemed tempted to scold her son. The question wasn't a very nice one. But she was curious about the answer, too.

Chief Brown reached into his pocket and pulled out the letters. The odor got even stronger as he fanned the papers out on the table.

"Onions!" Mrs. Brown proclaimed, holding her nose and blinking back tears. "The letters smell like onions." She looked more than a little relieved that the odor came from the letters and not her husband.

"It's peculiar," Chief Brown said. "This fellow claims he needs to drink a glass of onion juice every day for his health. I had to ask Max at the diner to make up a batch for him. Everything the thief touches smells like onions."

Encyclopedia blinked back a couple of onion tears.

His mother waited for him to ask the question that would solve the case.

The odor got even stronger as he fanned the paper out on the table.

But Encyclopedia didn't need to ask another question. He already had his answer.

"He might be a forgetful jewel thief," Encyclopedia said. "But if we read between the lines, we'll find out where he hid the jewels." He picked up one of the thief's letters. "All we need a 150-watt lightbulb."

WHY DID ENCYCLOPEDIA NEED A LIGHTBULB TO SOLVE THE CASE?

(Turn to page 81 for the solution to "The Case of the Forgetful Jewel Thief.")

The Case of the Autographed
Alice in Wonderland

Between schoolwork and police work, Encyclopedia kept busy during the winter. During the summer he ran his own detective agency in his family garage. He solved cases for the children of the neighborhood.

Every morning during the summer he hung his sign outside the garage:

BROWN DETECTIVE AGENCY
13 Rover Avenue
Leroy Brown, President
No case too small
25¢ per day
plus expenses

* * *

The first customer Friday morning was Melissa Stevens. Melissa was only five, and her favorite game was tea party. She set up a tea table in her front yard every afternoon and served tea to her dolls and stuffed animals.

"My Alice book is broken," she announced.

"Broken?" Encyclopedia asked. He had read more books than just about anybody, but never a broken one.

"Bugs Meany talked me into trading my Taffy the Tiger for it," Melissa said. "I didn't want to at first, but he said there was a tea party in the book. And that it was worth a whole bunch of money because the author signed it. But there's no tea party."

Bugs Meany was the leader of a gang of tough older boys. They called themselves the Tigers. They should have called themselves the Screwdrivers. They were always twisting the truth. Encyclopedia spent a lot of his time protecting the neighborhood kids from Bugs and his gang.

"There is a tea party in Lewis Carroll's *Alice in Wonderland*," Encyclopedia said with a smile. He reached for the book and flipped through a few pages. Half of the pictures had been cut out, and there were whole pages missing. "But you're right—it's not in this book."

Melissa's eyes widened. "Do you think the tiger thief tore up the book?"

Encyclopedia frowned. "Tiger thief?"

"Bugs said there was a tiger thief in town and Taffy wasn't safe," Melissa said. "I miss Taffy. I bet the author didn't even sign the book like Bugs said."

Encyclopedia turned to the front of the book. There was an autograph all right, but it wasn't the author's.

Melissa laid two quarters on the gas can beside Encyclopedia. "I want to hire you for two jobs—to get Taffy back from Bugs and to catch the tiger thief."

Encyclopedia gave her back one of her quarters. "I'll try to get Taffy back for you," he said. "But there is no tiger thief."

Melissa gasped. "Bugs lied?"

Encyclopedia nodded. "Bugs made that up to scare you into trading Taffy for his book."

"Can you get my Taffy back?"

"I'll do my best," Encyclopedia said. "We'd better go find Bugs."

"I have to tell you something very important," Melissa said nervously. She was afraid to go with him. "I'll stay here."

The detective talked Melissa into going with him. She had to identify Taffy.

The Tigers' clubhouse was an unused toolshed behind Mr. Sweeney's Auto Body Shop. The closer they came to it, the slower Melissa walked.

Bugs was sitting on an orange crate out front. Taffy stood at attention on the clubhouse roof.

"There he is," Melissa whispered. "And there's Taffy."

Upon seeing Encyclopedia, Bugs growled. "Scram before I hit you on the head so hard you'll blow your nose with your socks. This is Tiger land."

"Call the police," Melissa whispered. "All of them."

"We're here to get Melissa's tiger and give you back your book," Encyclopedia said.

Duke Kelly and Rocky Graham, two of Bugs Meany's Tigers, came out of the clubhouse and stood behind Bugs, sneering.

Bugs stood and puffed out his chest. "You two must have fallen down a rabbit hole and knocked your brains out," he said. "That book is signed by a famous author. It's worth a lot of money— way more than a silly stuffed tiger."

"Then you won't mind trading back," Encyclopedia said.

"No way," Bugs said. "A deal's a deal. Besides, I've gotten attached to Terrible Ted the Tiger. He's the mascot for our clubhouse."

Melissa stamped her little foot. "*Her* name is Taffy," she said.

"Well, he's mine now, and I can name *him* whatever I want," Bugs roared. "Besides, a book signed by the author is priceless. You could buy a hundred stuffed tigers for what that book is worth."

Melissa eyed Taffy longingly. "Maybe I should keep the book," she said. "If it's worth a lot of money."

"A storyteller signed this book," Encyclopedia said, "but it wasn't the author of *Alice in Wonderland*."

"You're crazy. That book was signed by the guy who wrote it." Bugs glared at Encyclopedia and Melissa. "Now get lost, bookworms. Slither back underground before I feed you to the birds."

Duke and Rocky laughed at Bugs's joke, but Melissa hid behind the detective again.

"I don't think he wants to be friends," Melissa said in a whisper.

Encyclopedia swallowed. It was three against one, but he had promised Melissa to get her tiger back. "You fooled Melissa with that phony story."

"You can't prove anything," Bugs said. "How do you know the author didn't sign that book?"

"If I can prove it," Encyclopedia asked, "will you give Melissa her tiger back?"

"Why not?"

Encyclopedia pulled a notebook and pen out

of his back pocket. "Would you write the author's name on this paper for me?"

Bugs eyed his Tiger friends with a smirk and swaggered up to Encyclopedia.

Melissa took a few steps back.

"You think I signed the book, but I didn't." Then Bugs grabbed the pen and wrote in big letters:

LOUIS CAROL

"See," he said, "the handwriting doesn't match."

The handwriting didn't match. But Encyclopedia had all the proof he needed. "A deal's a deal," he said. "Give Melissa back her tiger."

HOW DID ENCYCLOPEDIA PROVE THAT THE AUTHOR HADN'T SIGNED THE BOOK?

(Turn to page 82 for the solution to "The Case of the Autographed *Alice in Wonderland*.")

The Case of the Lemonade Stand

Bugs Meany hated being outsmarted by Encyclopedia all the time. He longed to get even. But every time he thought about giving Encyclopedia a mouth full of knuckles, he remembered Sally Kimball.

Sally was Encyclopedia's junior partner. She was also the prettiest girl and the best athlete in the fifth grade. What's more, she had done what no one—boy or girl—thought was possible. She had punched out Bugs Meany.

Bugs was trying to bully a little boy out of his bicycle the first time Sally knocked him silly. There was nothing Sally hated more than a bully.

"You need help," Sally said, dusting Bugs's chin with a straight right.

Bugs walked around like a boy who didn't know whether he was walking or riding. "I hope she isn't asking me to dance," he blubbered. Her punch had knocked him silly.

"Bugs doesn't like you any more than he likes me," Encyclopedia warned Sally. "His brain is working overtime on revenge."

"I'm not worried about anything he thinks up," Sally said. "His picture should be in the dictionary next to the word birdbrain."

The detectives were biking to the baseball field at South Park to watch their friends Fangs Liveright and Pinky Plummer play a Little League game. It was a hot ride.

"Let's stop for a cold drink," Sally said, spotting Sonia Easton's lemonade stand.

"Good idea," Encyclopedia agreed.

Sonia's lemonade stand was an Idaville landmark. She used it to raise money for the children's wing at the local hospital. Every year, she tried to top the year before.

"Two lemonades, please," Sally said, putting two dimes down on the counter.

"You're just in time," Sonia said, pouring two icy glasses of her famous thirst quencher. "I'm about to close up shop for a week. We're going to visit my cousins in Tallahassee."

"Won't that hurt business?" Encyclopedia asked.

"Not this year," Sonia said, pointing to a stack of coins and bills on the shelf behind her. "I'm way ahead of last year already."

Sally's forehead wrinkled in concern. "That's a lot of money to have sitting around. Shouldn't it be in a bank?"

"It's more than three hundred dollars!" Sonia said proudly. Then she explained. "The TV station was just here to do a story about me for the news. That's the only reason the money's here. Otherwise I keep it in the First National Bank."

Suddenly Sonia's eyes narrowed and she scowled. Encyclopedia looked over his shoulder. Bugs Meany was strolling by, listening to their conversation.

"That Bugs Meany," Sonia said. "He's never bought one glass of lemonade from me. But the minute the news crew showed up, he tried to get his ugly mug on television."

Sally shook her head. "Lucky he didn't break the camera."

A few minutes later, Sonia's mother came outside to hurry her along. Encyclopedia and Sally helped her carry her lemonade supplies into the house before they locked the stand's shutters and closed the side door Sonia used to get in and out.

Encyclopedia didn't think about Sonia again until early the next morning. He was eating his breakfast and reading about Fangs's home run in the *Idaville Morning News* when the phone rang.

The voice on the other end was high-pitched and muffled.

"Encyclopedia?"

"Yes," Encyclopedia answered.

"I forgot the money!"

"Who is this?" Encyclopedia asked.

"It's Sonia!" she said in a panicky voice. "I left all the money in the lemonade stand by accident. It's not safe!"

Encyclopedia strained to hear. Sonia's voice was barely understandable.

"I want to hire you to get it and keep it safe for me," she begged. "I called Sally already."

Encyclopedia was about to agree when the line went dead. A few minutes later, Sally coasted to a stop by the back door.

"Did Sonia call you?" she asked.

"Yes," said Encyclopedia, heading for his bike. "It was a terrible connection, but it sounded like she left all that money sitting inside the lemonade stand."

"We have to get it out of there before someone steals it," Sally said.

Encyclopedia hopped on his bike and pedaled

as fast as he could. Keeping up with Sally wasn't easy.

Sally pulled up alongside the lemonade stand and waited for Encyclopedia. He arrived a couple of minutes later, huffing and puffing.

"When did you get your pilot's license?" he asked, joking.

Sally shook her head. "You were driving way under the speed limit," she answered.

As soon as he could breathe, Encyclopedia understood why Sonia was so panicked. The lemonade stand's front shutters had a padlock, but the side door didn't have any kind of lock at all. Anyone could walk in and take the money.

He pushed the door open and stepped inside. "Did you bring a flashlight?" he asked Sally.

"No, I didn't think of it," she said, stepping in behind him and blocking the light from the door.

Encyclopedia took another step. The next thing he knew, a big fisherman's net dropped on top of him, trapping him inside. Sally struggled behind him. She was trapped, too.

Someone ran out from behind the stand and yelled at a passing police car. "Help, Officer! I've caught a couple of dangerous thieves."

Encyclopedia recognized the voice. It was Bugs Meany.

"I should have known Bugs was behind this," Sally muttered.

Encyclopedia watched Officer Muldoon walk toward them. The police officer helped Encyclopedia and Sally out of their trap.

All the while, Bugs was chattering in the background.

"The son of the police chief stealing money from sick kids," Bugs said, shaking his head sadly. "It's a disgrace!"

"What exactly were you doing here so early in the morning, Bugs?" Encyclopedia asked.

"I heard you two plotting to rob this place at the ball game last night," Bugs sneered. "Do you think I could stand by and let that happen? I

"Help, Officer! I've caught a couple of dangerous thieves!"

waited all night for you to step into my trap. I caught you red-handed."

"He's trying to frame us!" Sally said, rubbing her ankle. "We weren't going to steal the money. We were protecting it from people like him."

"People like me?" Bugs asked with a surprised expression. "I'm not the one trying to steal money from sick children." He turned to Officer Muldoon. "Call me as a star witness in the court case," he said. "Someone needs to lock these two up and throw away the key."

"Someone needs to give you a case of lockjaw," Sally said, making a fist.

Officer Muldoon eyed her sternly, and then turned to Bugs. "Tell me exactly what happened," he said, pulling out his notebook.

"I always suspected their little detective business was a front for a crime ring," Bugs said, puffing out his chest. "Then last night I heard them plotting to rob the lemonade stand. Money that was supposed to go to sick kids in the hospital."

Bugs put his hand over his heart. He seemed ready to weep phony tears down to his feet. "I knew no one would believe me over the police chief's son. So I laid a trap and hid here all night long. Sure enough, first thing this morning they crept in and grabbed the money. I caught them red-handed."

"Bugs Meany, that's the biggest lie you've ever told," Sally said, stamping her foot. "And you've told plenty of whoppers!"

Bugs ignored her and focused on Officer Muldoon. "I don't want a parade or a medal," Bugs said. "I just want those poor, sick kids to get every penny of that money."

He pulled a dime out of his pocket and added it to one of Sonia's neat stacks. "Here's another contribution from me."

"These are very serious charges," Officer Muldoon said. "I'm afraid I'm going to have to bring you all downtown and let your father sort it out, Leroy."

Sally was furious. "Encyclopedia," she cried. "Don't let Bugs get away with this!"

"He won't," Encyclopedia said calmly. "I can prove that Bugs is lying."

HOW?

(Turn to page 83 for the solution to "The Case of the Lemonade Stand.")

The Case of the
Revolutionary Treasures

Business was slow at the Brown Detective Agency. Encyclopedia and Sally were deciding whether to spend the afternoon at the beach or at the park when they heard a shout.

"The British are coming! The British are coming!"

They watched six-year-old Mark Goldberg race up the sidewalk on his scooter, waving a rusty lantern.

"Whoa, soldier," Encyclopedia said. "What's your hurry? You're late. The British came more than two hundred years ago."

"This was Paul Revere's!" Mark said, waving the lantern in front of Encyclopedia. "I just bought it. And after Wilford's book is published, I'm going to sell it for lots and lots of money. I'll be rich."

"Wilford Wiggins?" Encyclopedia asked. "He's lazier than a dead battery."

"He says he has to rest up before he gets tired," Sally added.

"He's not lazy," Mark said. "He's working on an important book about the war that made America, and he needs money to go to Philadelphia."

"You mean the American Revolution?" Sally asked.

Mark nodded.

Encyclopedia was starting to catch on. "So he's selling some historical treasures to get money for his trip?"

"Yup," Mark said. "And after his book is published all his stuff will be worth a ton of money."

Wilford was a high-school dropout. He spent his mornings under the covers and his afternoons trying to trick little kids out of their money. But his get-rich-quick schemes were usually bigger than his brains. Encyclopedia always stopped his phony deals in time.

"You'd better hurry," Mark said. "The auction starts at the city dump at two o'clock. Wilford did me a huge favor by selling me this light before the bidding started."

Encyclopedia took the lantern from Mark. "This is old all right, but if I believed it was Paul Revere's, I'd also believe that pigs could fly."

"You think it's a fake?" Mark asked.

Encyclopedia nodded. "How many times has Wilford Wiggins said he was going to make you rich?" he asked. "And how many times was he lying?"

"I believed him this time. Look how old this is. It's all rusty!" Mark shook his head sadly. "I emptied my piggy bank to buy this, or I'd hire you to get my money back."

"I just hired myself," Encyclopedia said. "If you get your money back, you can pay me a quarter." He turned to his junior partner. "We'd better get over there—"

Sally finished his sentence for him. "Before Wilford cheats the whole neighborhood out of their life savings."

Encyclopedia and Sally hopped on their bikes and headed to the dump, followed by Mark. He waved his lantern, only this time he cried, "The detectives are coming! The detectives are coming!"

Wilford was standing on a soapbox that looked all washed up. Another cardboard box sat at his side.

"Gather around," he said to a group of little kids. "I don't want to have to yell too loud and let the whole world know about the treasure—"

He broke off when he saw the detectives arrive with Mark.

He recovered quickly. "I guess everybody is welcome. Even nosy-bodies who weren't invited." Wilford pulled a stack of paper from the box and waved it in the air. "I've been working on a top-secret historical document for the past two years," Wilford said.

Sally grumbled at hearing the word "working" coming out of Wilford's mouth, but the other kids crowded in closer.

"I have collected some treasures from our country's great history during the course of my work, and I'm almost ready to publish my book—a *guaranteed* million-copy best seller." Wilford waved the papers, and repeated, "Million-copy best seller.

"But first," he went on, "I need to travel to Philadelphia, Pennsylvania, to gather one last fact. And what do you think I need to get there."

"Money?" Sally asked, sarcastically.

"Right!" Wilford ignored her tone of voice. "I need money to take my trip. So I have to give up my treasures. But I can guarantee each and every one of you," Wilford stopped and swept his eyes over his audience, "that these treasures will be worth ten times what you paid for them after my book is published. Museums will be begging to buy them from you for whatever price you ask."

Encyclopedia watched one little girl shake her piggy bank. Other children pulled quarters, dimes, nickels, and pennies out of their pockets.

Danny Lucas waved a ten-dollar bill in the air. "I was saving for a video game, but I can buy the whole video store when I sell Wilford's treasure."

Wilford's eyes lit up when he saw the bill. "Why, ten dollars will buy you my most important artifact. An original, handwritten letter from George Washington to his wife, Martha."

There was a gasp in the audience.

Wilford pulled a yellowed paper tube tied with a ribbon from the box and unrolled it to reveal the letter. "It's dated July 4, 1776, and begins: 'My dear Martha, I have just signed the Declaration of Independence.'"

Wilford cleared his throat importantly. "As we Revolutionary War historians know, the Americans had been fighting the British for many months before Thomas Jefferson wrote the Declaration. Every member of Congress signed it, including George Washington."

Encyclopedia opened his mouth to object. But Wilford cut him off. "Look how old and delicate this parchment is. It's the gen-u-ine thing, boys and girls. And no one can prove otherwise."

Sally took the letter from Wilford and scanned it. "It certainly looks old," she said to Encyclopedia. "Can Wilford be telling the truth?"

"No. He's lying, and I can prove it," Encyclopedia said.

HOW DID ENCYCLOPEDIA PROVE THE LETTER WAS A FAKE?

(Turn to page 84 for the solution to "The Case of the Revolutionary Treasures.")

The Case of the Missing Butterfly Brooch

The Browns' dinner table was quiet Thursday night. All the crimes in Idaville had been solved. Talk turned to the day's newspaper.

"Did you see the article about Mrs. Monarch's good luck in the *Idaville Morning News*?" Mrs. Brown asked.

Mrs. Monarch was known around town as the butterfly lady. She was crazy for butterflies. Her garden was filled with the kinds of flowers that attracted butterflies, like petunias, roses, and goldenrod.

The local Butterfly Gardener's Club often

met in her living room, where they could keep an eye on the many butterflies that sunned themselves in her front yard and fed on her flowers.

"I read the article," Chief Brown said. "Her aunt left her an antique butterfly brooch that turned out to be very valuable."

"That brooch will buy a lot of wildflowers if Mrs. Monarch decides to sell it," Encyclopedia added. "It's worth ten thousand dollars."

"I imagine she wants to keep it," Mrs. Brown said. "Her aunt was the person that got Mrs. Monarch interested in butterflies in the first place. It was something they shared. That butterfly pin is worth a lot more than money to her."

"I hope she locks that pin in a safe-deposit box at the bank," Chief Brown said. "A piece of jewelry that valuable shouldn't be kept in the house."

He had hardly finished his sentence before the doorbell rang.

"Who could that be?" Mrs. Brown asked.

Officer Lopez stood on the front porch with her hat in her hand. "Sorry to disturb your dinner, Chief," she said, after Encyclopedia led her into the dining room. "A masked man snuck into Mrs. Monarch's house while her butterfly club was meeting and stole her brooch. Mrs. Sweeney got a look at the back of him, but he jumped out a window with the brooch before she could alert anyone. Officer Rand is there now, but there don't seem to be any leads."

"Poor Mrs. Monarch," Mrs. Brown said. "She must be so upset—she loved that pin and the aunt who gave it to her."

Chief Brown shook his head. "I was just telling Leroy that that pin belonged in a bank," he said. "Every crook in the state could have read about that piece of jewelry in the newspaper today." He eyed the apple pie on the table and reached for his jacket.

Encyclopedia liked nothing more than going to crime scenes with his father. "Can I come with you?" he asked. "Maybe the thief left some clues behind."

"Is there any danger, dear?" Mrs. Brown asked.

"Leroy will be perfectly safe," the chief said. "And I'll take all the help I can get."

Mrs. Monarch's house was easy to spot. There was a butterfly painted on her mailbox and another on her front door.

Officer Rand met them on the porch. He had questioned the members of the Butterfly Gardener's Club. Aside from Mrs. Sweeney, no one had witnessed the crime, and so he sent them home.

A tearful Mrs. Monarch was wringing her hands. Her binoculars hung around her neck. "Thank goodness you've come, Chief Brown," she twittered. "I've never been so upset. My beautiful brooch—my most precious possession—is gone!"

Mrs. Sweeney patted her friend on the shoulder. "If only I hadn't been too stunned to scream," she said. "Someone might have gotten a good look at him."

Encyclopedia checked the picture window in the living room. It provided a perfect view of the oak tree in Mrs. Monarch's front yard. There were no butterflies in sight.

Encyclopedia remembered from a book on butterflies that they only flew in the sunlight. On cloudy days and when it was dark they rested underneath leaves and on tree bark. They liked to blend into their surroundings to protect themselves from flying predators.

Officer Rand led the group upstairs while Mrs. Sweeney explained what happened. "Mrs. Monarch and the rest of the club were watching a particularly fine redbanded hairstreak perch on a leaf before settling down for the night when I went upstairs to use the restroom. I had just gotten to the top of the stairs when I saw a masked man in Mrs. Monarch's bedroom." Mrs. Sweeney shuddered, remembering.

"I'll never forget that look in his eyes when

he saw me," she said. "He was such a pro that he didn't make a sound. He must have climbed down the farside of the tree. No one in the living room saw him."

Officer Rand finished the story as they stepped into Mrs. Monarch's bedroom. "By the time Mrs. Sweeney came to her senses, the masked man was long gone—and so was Mrs. Monarch's brooch. He could be anywhere by now."

"I feel terrible," Mrs. Sweeney said. "Can you dust for fingerprints?" she asked, rubbing her hands together. "Could the thief have given himself away when he touched the window?"

"Only if his fingerprints are already on file," the chief answered.

Mrs. Sweeney's shoulders slumped. Mrs. Monarch watched a whip-poor-will fly by and imitated its lonesome song with a sigh.

The thief had rifled through Mrs. Monarch's drawers and her jewelry box. "Has anything else been taken?" Chief Brown asked.

Suddenly, about a hundred butterflies took to the air flapping their wings in alarm.

"No, just my butterfly brooch," Mrs. Monarch chirped. "I blame myself. I never should have talked to that newspaper reporter."

Encyclopedia noticed Officer Rand's powerful flashlight underneath the bedroom window. A large branch was within his reach. Encyclopedia shook it back and forth and shined the flashlight on the tree. Suddenly, about a hundred butterflies took to the air flapping their wings in alarm.

"I'd do anything to get my brooch back," Mrs. Monarch said. "Should I offer a reward?"

"We'll send notices to all the jewelry stores in the state," Chief Brown said. "When the thief tries to sell the pin, we'll catch him."

"That won't be necessary, Dad," Encyclopedia said. "I know who has the brooch."

WHO WAS THE THIEF?

(Turn to page 85 for the solution to "The Case of the Missing Butterfly Brooch.")

The Case of the Counterfeit Dough

The morning of the Idaville Cookie Bake-off, Joey Perkins, Encyclopedia's classmate, walked into the Brown Detective Agency.

"I need your help," he said, placing a quarter on the red gasoline can. "I have three recipes for chocolate-chip cookies. I want to hire you to tell me which one is best."

"You can pay me to eat your cookies anytime," Encyclopedia said.

Sally agreed. "But what are you worried about?" she asked. "You're sure to win the bake-off this year."

Joey's cookies had come in second to Christina Vargas's three years in a row in the twelve and under class. But Christina had turned thirteen in June. No one else's sweet treats would come close to Joey's in a taste test.

"There's a new twelve-year-old baker in town, Mary Macaroon," Joey said. "Her cousin is one of the judges, and she's tough. My cookies have to be perfect."

"I heard that this year's first prize is fifty dollars, and the winning recipe will be printed in a cookbook," Sally said.

Joey nodded. "I've always dreamed of having my recipes published."

He placed a plate with six cookies on the workbench—three cookies for each detective. Then he handed them water bottles so that they could rinse their mouths after tasting each one.

The detectives munched on the delicious cookies, carefully rinsing their mouths after each taste.

"Yum," said Sally, "they're all delicious."

"What's this in cookie number two?" Encyclopedia asked. "A hint of cinnamon?"

Joey shook his head with a grin. "It's a secret," he said. "I won't tell."

"They're all winners," Encyclopedia said. "But I like cookie number two best."

Sally took another bite of cookie number three. Then she tasted cookie number two again. "Cookie number two it is," she said.

"I sure hope I win this year," Joey said, picking up his plate and heading down the driveway. "I want a first place ribbon and my cookie recipe in that cookbook!"

"We'll be there to cheer you on," Encyclopedia said.

"Good luck!" Sally called after him.

Later that afternoon, Encyclopedia and Sally biked to the high school. The bake-off was being held in the school's kitchen. Four tables were set out for the contestants in the twelve and under category. Each table held flour, sugar, butter, eggs, chocolate chips, and a few spices like cinnamon and nutmeg.

Encyclopedia and Sally watched Joey measure his ingredients carefully and mix his cookie dough.

Two of the contestants—Emily Drew and Michael Esposito—each seemed to be making more of a mess than a cookie. Flour flew when Michael tried to mix his dough, sprinkling the judges and making them sneeze.

Mary Macaroon looked like a serious challenger. She even wore an official chef's hat and apron.

"Fashion doesn't win bake-offs," Sally said with a sniff.

But Encyclopedia noticed that she whisked her eggs and creamed her butter and sugar like a pro.

Joey was the first to slide his cookie sheets into the oven, followed by Mary. Soon the smell of baking cookies filled the room. Encyclopedia's mouth watered.

Ten minutes later, four oven timers buzzed,

one after the other. As soon as all four trays of cookies were on the table, the judges took out their clipboards. They stopped at Michael Esposito's table first.

Each of the three judges carefully chewed one of his cookies, making notes about the crispness of the baked dough or the sweetness of the chocolate. When all three were finished, an assistant handed them glasses of water. The judges swished water around their mouths and then swallowed.

"They're clearing their taste buds for the next cookie," Sally remarked.

The judges went through the same routine with Emily Drew's cookies. Then they stood in front of Mary Macaroon.

"They're taking extra bites of Mary's cookies," Sally noticed. "They must be good."

"Not too good, I hope," Encyclopedia said, watching closely. "Getting his recipe published is Joey's dream."

The judges finished with Mary's cookies and motioned for the assistant to bring them fresh water. They rinsed their mouths and emptied their glasses. Judge number two filled her glass again. Then all three stepped in front of Joey's table.

Joey nervously chewed on his lip. He watched the judges pick up his cookies. His mouth opened and closed with theirs as they each took a bite.

The judges coughed and sputtered. One spit Joey's cookie into a napkin. Judge number two quickly downed her water as the assistant rushed forward with filled glasses for the other judges.

Joey's face fell in dismay. He took a bite of one of his cookies, and then spit it out again. "I don't know what happened," he cried. "This tastes awful!"

Encyclopedia stepped forward and took a small nibble. He sniffed the cinnamon on Joey's table. Then he shook some sugar into his hand and tasted it. "Someone's substituted salt for your sugar, and red pepper for cinnamon," he said.

Joey's shoulders slumped. "I won't even be number two this year," he moaned. "I'll be last."

Encyclopedia turned to the judges. "Can you let everyone start over, with fresh ingredients?"

"That's not fair to the other contestants," judge number two said sternly. "We need to award the prize."

"That's easy for you to say," Encyclopedia said. "You were the one who rigged the ingredients."

HOW DID ENCYCLOPEDIA KNOW?

(Turn to page 86 for the solution to "The Case of the Counterfeit Dough.")

The Case of the
Astronaut Duck

Encyclopedia and his pal Charlie Stewart had a watermelon-seed spitting contest after lunch. Sally used a tape measure to determine the winner. Encyclopedia was ahead by three inches.

Suddenly, Moonboy Webster ran by wearing his astronaut helmet.

Moonboy Webster, whose real name was Austin, was Idaville's astronaut-in-training. He'd been talking about rocketing to the stars ever since he witnessed his first space shuttle launch. He walked, talked, ate, and dreamed about nothing but outer space.

"Did you hear?" he called excitedly from the end of the driveway. "There's a real NASA astronaut right here in Idaville!"

That got Encyclopedia's attention. He liked to learn about outer space, too.

"He's raising money for a space mission," Moonboy said. "He's going to talk at the town hall about being an astronaut!"

Sally's eyes lit up. "Let's go hear him speak," she said.

"He's charging fifty cents," Moonboy told them. "I just ran home to get my money. The talk starts in ten minutes."

Encyclopedia kept the money he earned from his detective business in a shoe box. He hid the shoe box behind an old tire in the garage. Every Friday, he and Sally took the week's earnings to the bank.

Luckily, today was Thursday. There was enough money in the shoe box for the two detectives and Charlie to attend the talk without having to stop at the bank. They walked downtown with Moonboy, who chattered about space.

"This is more popular than a free trip to the circus," Sally said, eyeing the long line in front of the town hall.

The detectives and their friends shuffled forward as one by one kids from all over Idaville handed their coins to a man wearing a NASA T-shirt.

As soon as the man had collected everyone's money, he walked to the front of the auditorium and climbed to the stage.

Moonboy fired questions like rocket boosters from his front-row seat. He was too excited to even wait for the answers.

"Did you work on the Mars mission?

"Are moon rocks heavy?

"Have you ever been to the space station?

"Is zero gravity really cool?"

Finally, the astronaut jumped in. "I'll take questions after my talk," he said. "But now I want to tell you all about a new space mission.

It's top secret, so I'm only sharing it with you. And you have to promise to keep it that way." He swept his eyes over all the children in the audience. "Top secret," he said gravely.

Moonboy's eyes got wide. "Top secret," he whispered.

Encyclopedia watched the kids around him nod yes as they waited for the astronaut to share his secret.

Pictures of men in space were projected onto the screen behind him as the astronaut spoke.

"I've gone on many missions for NASA," he said. "I've traveled through space. I've conducted experiments on the International Space Station. I've even walked in space.

"Now I'm ready," he announced solemnly, "to travel to another galaxy. To find planets that no human has ever seen, even through a telescope."

A diagram of a spaceship unlike anything the kids had ever seen was shown on the screen. It was round and flat, like a flying saucer, and it had a small pool next to the pilot's seat.

"And I will take just one companion as I travel through space."

The astronaut took a dramatic pause and reached behind a curtain. A duck wearing a little space helmet waddled onto the stage. There were gasps from the audience. Encyclopedia heard a muffled quack from behind the helmet.

"An astronaut duck!" Moonboy said, jumping to his feet.

Other kids in the audience laughed and clapped. No one had ever heard of a duck in space.

"I could go into a lot of details about aerodynamics and space and how many years of my life will be devoted to this great mission," the astronaut said, "but I know you all really want to know about this wonderful duck."

Encyclopedia raised his eyebrows. "I've got to hear this," he said.

Moonboy bit his lips to keep from asking the astronaut a million questions.

A series of pictures continued to flash behind

*Other kids in the audience laughed and clapped. No one had
ever heard of a duck in space.*

the astronaut as he talked about the duck. "This astronaut duck has been to the moon. He's been to the space station. He's even walked in space!"

The astronaut took the duck's helmet off and a loud quack echoed through the auditorium.

"I need a volunteer to take care of this brave astronaut duck while I raise money for my mission," the astronaut said. "There must be one child here who would do this for his country."

Moonboy jumped to his feet. But he was surrounded by a chorus of other kids volunteering to take the duck.

"And, of course, I'll need a small fee of fifty dollars," the astronaut said.

"Fifty dollars!" the kids cried. Most of them sat right back down. But Moonboy stayed on his feet.

"It'll take every penny I have saved, but I'll get the money," Moonboy said.

The astronaut seemed relieved and happy, until Encyclopedia got to his feet.

"Save your money, Moonboy," he said. "And,

you," he said to the man, "better give us back our fifty cents. You're not an astronaut. You're a fake."

HOW DID ENCYCLOPEDIA KNOW?

(Turn to page 87 for the solution to "The Case of the Astronaut Duck.")

The Case of the Lucky Catch

Encyclopedia and some of the gang were on their way to a picnic. Ace Harvey, a retired major-league baseball player, invited all of Idaville's Little League teams to his estate near the beach.

Encyclopedia, Pinky Plummer, Billy and Jody Turner, Herb Stein, Charlie Stewart, and Sally Kimball took the number nine bus. They carried baseballs, gloves, and bats that they hoped Mr. Harvey would autograph.

"Do you think we'll get to see the baseball?" Pinky asked.

No one had to ask what baseball. Ace Harvey had made the most famous catch in baseball history. He made the game-winning catch in the ninth inning of the seventh game of the World Series. Not only did his team win the game, they became world champions with just one catch.

After the game, he had every single one of his teammates sign his lucky ball. Mr. Harvey had been offered thousands of dollars for his baseball, but he refused to sell.

"I hope we do get to see the ball," Billy Turner said. "I'd love to hold it in my hand for just one second. Do you think it would bring me good luck?"

Everyone knew that Billy's team had lost a big game when Billy dropped a high fly. Ever since, he didn't seem to be able to catch a ball. He even dropped the ball when he was pitching! He was in a real slump.

"You need more than luck," Jody teased. "You need a new sport."

Sally shushed Jody with a look, then turned to Billy. "I hear he keeps the ball locked up in a glass case," she said. "But maybe just looking at it will break you out of your slump."

"Then I'll look at it until my eyes hurt," Billy said, ignoring his twin.

The bus stopped on Mr. Harvey's corner and the children got off. The friends were suddenly shy when they got a look at Ace Harvey's mansion. It was one of the biggest in Idaville. Then Encyclopedia rang the doorbell. It played *Take Me Out to the Ball Game*, and they all relaxed.

A maid answered and led Encyclopedia and his pals through a center hall toward the backyard. On the way, they passed the glass case. A spotlight shone on the game-winning baseball. The ball turned on its pedestal so that they could see every autograph. Billy stared at it without blinking.

Then the friends were led to the back door. Ace Harvey shook hands with everyone and signed their balls, bats, and gloves. He waved them into the backyard, which was already filled with kids playing catch on the baseball diamond, splashing in the pool, or eating as many hot dogs and hamburgers as they could fit in their stomachs.

Mr. Harvey had hired a baseball coach, lifeguards, barbecue chefs, and even a games director to make sure everyone had a good time.

Billy flopped in the grass next to Encyclopedia and Sally. The detectives had just won a three-legged race.

"I can't get my mind off Ace Harvey's baseball," Billy said. "Do you think if I asked as a special favor he'd let me hold it?"

Encyclopedia looked at his friend. Billy had dropped his egg in the egg-carrying contest and there was dried yolk all over his shirt. "You can ask," Encyclopedia said. "But holding someone else's baseball won't break your slump. All you need to get your confidence back is one good catch."

"Catch?" Billy groaned. "I can't catch my reflection in the mirror." He got to his feet. "I'm going to go and stare at the ball some more."

Encyclopedia entered the relay race with Pinky and Charlie, and he forgot all about Billy until he saw two police cars pull into Ace Harvey's driveway. His father waved and then headed into the house.

Encyclopedia went inside to see what was up. Mr. Harvey had a tight grip on Billy's left arm and was talking to Chief Brown.

The baseball case was broken. A few bits of glass lay scattered on the pedestal, and the baseball was nowhere to be seen.

Three officers were searching the rooms on the first floor.

Billy's eyes darted from Chief Brown to Mr. Harvey and back again. He held his right hand in front of him, palm up. It was bleeding. He tried not to let it drip on Mr. Harvey's floor.

"I found this hooligan in front of the case. The glass was broken and my baseball is gone."

Mr. Harvey said. "He won't tell me where he hid it, so I called you."

"I didn't take it," Billy moaned. "I just came in to look at it again, and it was gone. There was glass everywhere. I cut my hand, and then Mr. Harvey came in and started yelling."

Encyclopedia heard a gasp behind him. Other kids from the picnic had followed him into the house.

"He kept saying he wanted to hold that ball," Charlie muttered.

"Billy, you didn't . . ." Sally said.

"You can't trust any friends of brainhead Brown," Bugs Meany shouted. "Give up the ball, Billy. Tell the cops where it is."

"But I didn't steal it," Billy said again.

Chief Brown asked Officer Lopez to take Billy into the bathroom for some first aid. The other officers led the kids back outside.

"Can I stay, Dad?" Encyclopedia asked.

His father nodded. "Do you have any information that might help us, Leroy?"

"I know Billy was in a slump," Encyclopedia said. "But I don't believe he'd try to steal Mr. Harvey's baseball."

"Well that's exactly what he did," Mr. Harvey insisted. "I found him standing in front of the case with a bleeding hand." Mr. Harvey shook his head. "He must have hidden the baseball with a plan to come back for it later.

"It's a good thing I just insured that baseball," Mr. Harvey continued. "It's worth thousands of dollars."

"It looks bad for your friend, Leroy," Chief Brown said. "Do you think you can get him to tell you where he hid the baseball?"

Encyclopedia looked into the case again. There were pieces of glass all over the bottom and on the pedestal that had held the baseball just this morning. "Can I ask a question first?"

His father nodded.

Encyclopedia turned to Mr. Harvey. "How many people have keys to the case?" he asked.

"I have the only key," Mr. Harvey answered.

"I unlock the case for the maid when the glass needs cleaning."

"There's no need to question Billy, Dad," Encyclopedia said. "Mr. Harvey is the only one that can tell us where the ball is hidden."

HOW DID ENCYCLOPEDIA KNOW?

(Turn to page 88 for the solution to "The Case of the Lucky Catch.")

The Case of the Missing Money

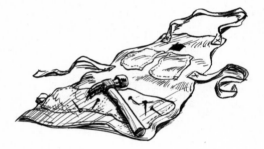

On Saturday, Encyclopedia and his father headed to the west side of town to help build houses.

An organization called Shelter from the Storm was building three houses on what used to be a farmer's field. Where tomatoes and cucumbers once grew, families who lost their homes in hurricanes would be putting down roots of a different kind.

A busy team of volunteers was already at work. Encyclopedia and Mr. Brown grabbed their hammers and walked up to the chief carpenter to get their tasks.

Patrick Freeman wore a carpenter's apron that had a small picture of a house in the center. The apron held all kinds of tools, including nails and a tape measure in the two front pockets. A hammer hung from the loop on the apron's right side.

Mr. Freeman thanked the Browns for coming and pointed to two other carpenters. Both wore carpenter's aprons with the same picture. "That's Fred," he said. Fred was framing the walls on house number two.

"And there's Dan."

Dan was showing a group of volunteers how to put up wallboard.

"If you get into any trouble, be sure to ask one of us to lend a hand," Mr. Freeman said.

Encyclopedia and his father spent the first half of the morning helping to frame a house. The volunteers were amazed at how quickly a house could be built when so many people worked together.

It was hot, thirsty work. Encyclopedia took a break and ran into Mr. Freeman by the water

table. A car was just driving away, and Encyclopedia noticed Mr. Freeman slip a twenty dollar
bill into an inside pocket on his apron.

"The folks in Idaville sure are generous," he
said. "People keep stopping by to give me donations. At this rate, we'll be able to build three
more houses next weekend."

A few minutes later, their house was framed
and Mr. Freeman showed Encyclopedia's team
how to hammer down the floorboards. He
grabbed a nail from his front left pocket and
reached for his hammer.

"You want to use a firm grip," he said, demon-
strating. "And hit the nail right in the center."

Encyclopedia watched him drive the nail in,
then reach for another nail, then another.

All three houses were well on their way to
being finished by lunchtime. The front porch
was already in place on house number one.

Encyclopedia and his father sat at a portable
picnic table with the rest of the volunteers while
Mr. Freeman and his carpenters inspected the

morning's work. Encyclopedia kept his eyes on them while he unpacked the ham and cheese sandwiches, apples, and cookies that Mrs. Brown had made for him and his father. He watched Dan remove a crooked nail and hammer a new one in its place with the same easy rhythm as Mr. Freeman.

The carpenters seemed satisfied. They hung their aprons over the porch railing of house number one and joined the volunteers for lunch. Mr. Freeman entertained the crowd with stories of building houses all over the country.

"Once, in Idaho, we discovered that we were erecting a house in a field full of snakes," he said with a laugh. "Boy, did we change our location— and fast."

"Have you ever been as far away as Alaska?" Encyclopedia asked.

"Sure have," Dan said. "I've built houses in every one of the fifty states."

Fred was brand new to the carpentry field. "I've only been in a couple of states so far," he said. "I'm looking forward to seeing the rest of the country."

While they were eating, three more people stopped by with donations. It seemed like anyone from Idaville who wasn't on the building site with a hammer in his or her hand stopped by with money to help build more houses.

After lunch, everyone cleaned up their garbage and grabbed their hammers. Dan and Fred put their carpenters' aprons back on and showed the volunteers how to raise the walls on house number two. Mr. Freeman stepped into his trailer to take care of some paperwork.

Chief Brown and Encyclopedia held a wall in place. Dan fumbled reaching for his nails and almost hammered a hole in the middle of his tape measure with his left hand.

A few minutes later, they heard a cry. Mr. Freeman stood in front of house number one with his carpenter's apron.

Chief Brown rushed over, followed by Encyclopedia.

"Someone's stolen the donations," Mr. Freeman said. "I put them in an inside pocket in my apron, and now they're gone."

"Are you sure that's your apron?" Chief Brown asked.

Mr. Freeman examined it again. "It sure looks like mine. But new Shelter from the Storm aprons were issued to us just last month, and they all look the same."

Fred and Dan came over as soon as they could get away. Chief Brown asked to see their aprons. Mr. Freeman was right. They were exactly the same. The inside pockets of all three aprons were empty.

"Hundreds of dollars—gone!" Mr. Freeman shook his head. "That money would have helped build new houses for people who need them."

"One of the volunteers must have taken the money," Dan said.

Chief Brown surveyed the group, who were still busy hammering, sawing, and building. "The aprons were in plain view all during

"Someone's stolen the donations," Mr. Freeman said.

lunch," he said. "If someone picked up an apron and removed a stack of bills, they would have been seen."

Encyclopedia cleared his throat.

"Did you see something, Leroy?" Chief Brown asked.

"Are you left-handed?" he asked Mr. Freeman.

"No, I'm right-handed," he asked with a puzzled expression.

Fred looked worried and confused. "Chief Brown, don't you think you had better start questioning the volunteers?" he asked. "What if the thief sneaks away?"

"You don't have to do that, Dad," Encyclopedia said. "I can tell you who took the money."

ENCYCLOPEDIA KNEW WHO TOOK THE MONEY. DO YOU?

(Turn to page 89 for the solution to "The Case of the Missing Money.")

The Case of the Stolen Confederate Stamps

Encyclopedia's stomach rumbled. He put down his book and checked his watch. It was ten minutes past dinnertime, and no one had called him to the table.

He followed the smell of spaghetti and meatballs to the kitchen.

"Your father will be a little late tonight," Mrs. Brown said. "He's tied up with a case at the convention center."

Encyclopedia's eyes lit up at the prospect of a case. "Do you think Dad needs help?" he asked. Then his stomach rumbled again.

"Your stomach and your curiosity will have

to wait a few more minutes," Mrs. Brown said.

At half past six, Chief Brown came home.

"What's happening at the convention center this week?" Mrs. Brown asked, after he had washed up and sat down at the table.

"The Philatelic Society is having its annual convention," he answered.

"The stamp collectors," Encyclopedia said. "Sally and I plan to bike there tomorrow and look at the new stamps."

"Two very old stamps were stolen this afternoon," Chief Brown said. "We recovered them, but we don't know who stole them."

"Give Leroy all the details," Mrs. Brown said. "He's helped you out before."

Chief Brown pulled his notebook out of his pocket with a sigh. "I don't know," he said. "Even Leroy might have trouble with this case. It's got me licked."

Encyclopedia ate his spaghetti while he waited for the details.

"A dealer named Mr. Sansbury brought two rare stamps to the show," Chief Brown said.

"Both were issued by the Confederate government after the Civil War began. The first was a five-cent green Jefferson Davis stamp. The second was a ten-cent stamp with a picture of Thomas Jefferson."

"There must be lots of suspects," Mrs. Brown said.

"No." Chief Brown shook his head. "Mr. Sansbury didn't put these stamps on display. He kept them locked in a small office. But he gave three collectors, all of them longtime friends, the key to the office so they could view the stamps in private. They each spent time alone in the room before Mr. Sansbury noticed the stamps were missing."

"But you said you already found the stamps," Mrs. Brown said. "Didn't they also lead you to the thief?"

"We searched each of the three suspects thoroughly," Chief Brown answered. "Then Officer Lopez discovered that someone had pried up a corner of the carpet and slipped the stamps underneath. The thief must have intended to go back for the stamps at a later date. But it's impossible to find out which one of the three is the real thief."

Mrs. Brown glanced at Encyclopedia. She seemed a little disappointed that he hadn't solved the mystery yet.

"Tell us about the suspects," she prodded.

Chief Brown turned the pages of his notebook. "Each one of the suspects was alone in the room for a short time. The first was a Mr. Beckman from Tampa. He told us that he already had these stamps in his collection, a fact that Mr. Sansbury was able to confirm.

"Mrs. Dwyer is planning to open a stamp museum and store in the northern part of the state. But she couldn't believe that a serious stamp collector would hide such valuable stamps on a damp concrete floor where they could be damaged."

"Perhaps it was the third suspect," Mrs. Brown said.

"That may be," Chief Brown said. "Mr. Patterson has a well-known album of early Ameri-

can and Confederate stamps. And he has long
been searching for these two to complete his
collection."

Mrs. Brown looked at Encyclopedia. She had
run out of questions herself and hoped he was
ready to ask the one that would truly crack the
case.

Suddenly his eyes opened. "What kind of carpet was on the floor?" he asked.

"A standard dark blue carpet for a place like
the convention center where there's lots of foot
traffic," Chief Brown answered. "The thief had
pulled up one corner."

Encyclopedia opened his eyes. "Then it's
obvious who the thief is, it's . . ."

WHO WAS IT?

(Turn to page 90 for the solution to "The Case of the
Stolen Confederate Stamps.")

Solution to *The Case of the Forgetful Jewel Thief*

The jewel thief was forgetful. Mrs. Brown suspected he might have written his hiding places down, and she was right. As soon as Encyclopedia learned about the onion juice he was able to shed some light on the situation.

Onion juice can be used as an invisible ink. The words, but not the smell, disappear as soon as the juice dries on the paper. Encyclopedia realized that while the thief had used a regular pen to write what seemed like ordinary letters, in between the lines, he wrote with onion juice. The thief knew that his mother would keep all his letters. She never dreamed of the secrets they contained.

Encyclopedia and his father carefully heated the letters under a 150-watt lightbulb until the secret writing appeared. Each letter revealed a hiding place for a secret stash of jewels.

Chief Brown called the police chiefs in each and every town, and soon all of the stores had their jewels back.

Solution to *The Case of the Autographed Alice in Wonderland*

Bugs may not have signed the book, but he gave away his trick when he penned the author's name for Encyclopedia. He got the name right, but he spelled it wrong. *Alice in Wonderland* was written by Lewis Carroll, not Louis Carol.

When confronted with the proof, Bugs admitted that he saw Taffy on Melissa's front lawn and thought the tiger would make a great mascot for his clubhouse. He went home, found the old book, and had Rocky sign it with the author's name. He made up the tiger thief story when Melissa didn't want to trade.

If Bugs's baby cousin hadn't cut pictures out of the book and ripped out the title page, they would have known the correct spelling of Lewis Carroll.

Luckily for Melissa, they didn't.

Bugs gave back Taffy the Tiger and apologized—gritting his teeth the whole time.

Solution to *The Case of the Lemonade Stand*

Bugs wanted to get even with the boy detective who always outsmarted him. He wanted revenge on Sally who always out punched him.

He watched the detectives help Sonia close up her lemonade stand and noticed that no one locked up the money. He pretended to be Sonia on the phone. Then he watched as the detectives walked right into his trap.

Bugs's plan might have worked except for one thing. He talked too much.

Bugs said that he caught Encyclopedia and Sally redhanded. Later he said that he watched them grab the money.

But that was impossible.

If Bugs had really caught the pair "red-handed," the money would still be in their hands when Encyclopedia and Sally were swept up in Bugs's trap. The money was still stacked neatly on the shelf when Bugs added his dime.

When Encyclopedia pointed out the flaw in Bugs's story, the bully confessed.

Officer Muldoon drove beside Encyclopedia and Sally as they biked to the First National Bank. They deposited the money in Sonia's account.

Solution to *The Case of the Revolutionary Treasures*

Encyclopedia knew Wilford Wiggins was no historian with a million-copy best seller up his sleeve. But he didn't know how to prove it until Wilford brought out his "most important artifact"—George Washington's letter to Martha Washington.

Encyclopedia knew something Wilford didn't. George Washington wasn't one of the signers of the Declaration of Independence. As Commander-in-Chief of the Continental Army, he was in New York fighting the British, not in Philadelphia signing the Declaration.

When Encyclopedia pointed out this truth to Wilford, he admitted that all of his "revolutionary antiques" were fakes. For the letter, he soaked a piece of paper in tea to make it look old. Then he added the words and the signature himself.

The neighborhood kids kept their money, and Wilford gave Mark Goldberg his savings back. Mark got to keep the rusty lantern, too, just in case the British ever decided to invade Idaville.

Solution to *The Case of the Missing Butterfly Brooch*

Encyclopedia suspected Mrs. Sweeney the minute she asked about fingerprints. Her shoulders slumped in relief, not sadness, when Chief Brown told her the thief's fingerprints would only be useful if the thief's prints were on file.

But Encyclopedia was sure as soon as he flashed the light on the tree outside the window. Mrs. Sweeney said the crook had climbed down the tree. But if that were true, Mrs. Monarch and the other club members in the living room would have been alerted to trouble when the butterflies took flight. And they would have seen the masked man through their binoculars.

When confronted with Encyclopedia's theory, Mrs. Sweeney admitted to slipping the brooch into her pocket.

Mrs. Sweeney left the Butterfly Gardener's Club and Idaville in disgrace, and Mrs. Monarch put the butterfly brooch in the bank—except for very special occasions.

Solution to *The Case of the*
Counterfeit Dough

An assistant brought fresh water to the judges *after* each tasting. But Encyclopedia noticed that judge number two made sure her water glass was full *before* tasting Joey's cookie. She knew it would taste awful and wanted to have a glass of water at the ready.

When confronted with the evidence, she confessed. Judge number two wanted her cousin Mary to win the contest and was afraid Joey's cookies would be impossible to beat.

She was right. Joey remixed his cookie dough with the right ingredients. He walked away with the blue ribbon for first prize, a check for fifty dollars, and a chance to have his recipe published in a cookbook.

Solution to *The Case of the Astronaut Duck*

Encyclopedia wondered why a real NASA astronaut would have to raise money from schoolkids, fifty cents at a time. He suspected the astronaut was a fake the minute he started talking about top secret missions. But he didn't know for sure until he saw the duck.

If that duck had truly flown in space, it wouldn't have lived to quack the tale. Ducks need gravity to swallow. It would have starved in a weightless space capsule.

The man admitted that he was a phony. He was simply trying to make some fast money and pretending to be an astronaut was his latest scam. When he came across a doll's space helmet—the perfect size to fit a duck—he got the idea for an astronaut duck. He used a computer to put the duck into the pictures so it would look like the duck had flown in space.

The man set the duck free, and Moonboy kept the fifty dollars he was saving for space camp.

Solution to *The Case of the Lucky Catch*

Encyclopedia noticed a clue that his father had missed.

There was glass sitting on the small pedestal in place of the baseball. If someone had broken the glass case and then taken the baseball, the pedestal would not have had broken glass on it.

Ace Harvey wanted to collect the insurance money and keep his baseball as well. Billy Turner was just in the wrong place at the wrong time. When Mr. Harvey walked in and found him with a piece of glass in his hand, he decided to frame him for the robbery.

When Encyclopedia stated his theory, Mr. Harvey confessed. A couple of weeks later, he sold the ball to a baseball museum. By the next spring, he had moved out of Idaville.

After Billy's hand healed, he started catching fly balls again.

Solution to *The Case of the Missing Money*

Dan was an experienced carpenter who had built houses in all fifty states. But after lunch he started fumbling and almost destroyed a tape measure. Encyclopedia realized that was because Dan was left-handed. He normally kept his nails in the right pocket of his apron, leaving his left hand free to hold the hammer. But the nails in the apron he wore after lunch were on the left side. The apron belonged to a right-handed carpenter.

Dan had watched Mr. Freeman put money into his apron all morning long. When his boss stepped into the trailer after lunch, Dan decided to switch aprons. He slipped the money out of the apron and into his pocket when no one was looking. But his fumbling for nails gave him away. Both Mr. Freeman and Fred were right-handed and kept their nails on the opposite side of the apron as the left-handed carpenter.

When Encyclopedia laid out the facts, Dan confessed and returned the money.

Solution to *The Case of the Stolen Confederate Stamps*

As soon as his father said the carpet was standard for a place like the convention center, Encyclopedia realized it had to have been a wall-to-wall carpet. Only the person who pulled up the carpet would know what the floor was like underneath. Mrs. Dwyer gave herself away when she said that she would never hide the stamps on a damp concrete floor.

After dinner, Chief Brown and Encyclopedia confronted her and she confessed. She did worry about damaging the valuable stamps on the floor. But the Confederate stamps would have drawn a lot of people into her museum and store, so she decided to take her chances. She planned to return to the convention center and retrieve the stamps after the show was over.